ADVENTURES IN THE KINGDOM™

SECRET OF THE BLUE POUCH

Written by Dian Layton.
Illustrations created by Al Berg.

Illustrations created by Al Berg.

Published by MercyPlace Ministries

MercyPlace is a licensed imprint of Destiny Image®, Inc.

Distributed by

Destiny Image® Publishers, Inc.
P.O. Box 310
Shippensburg, PA 17257-0310

ISBN 0-9677402-7-4

For Worldwide Distribution
Printed in the U.S.A.

This book and all other Destiny Image, Revival Press, MercyPlace, Fresh Bread, and Treasure House books are available at Christian bookstores and distributors worldwide.

For a U.S. bookstore nearest you, call **1-800-722-6774**.
For more information on foreign distributors, call **717-532-3040**.
Or reach us on the Internet: **www.seeker.org**

CONTENTS

Glee

Gladness

Giggles

Do

Doodle

Seeker

Dawdle

Yes

Slow

HopeSo

KnowSo

Lurking in the shadows somewhere between the CARNALville of Selfishness and the Kingdom of Joy and Peace was a dragon.

He appeared to be small and unimportant; but this dragon was actually more evil and more cunning than many other dragons.

As he sneaked through bushes and trees, the dragon was singing his lifesong, "I have worked so hard, and I deserve the best; it's only fair and right—that I have more, not less...."

The dragon's name was Itsalmine.

Earlier that day, Itsalmine had met with the dragon-clowns and their master in the deep dark place beneath the trap door of the CARNALville of Selfishness. It was agreed that he would be the perfect dragon to send on a very important assignment. His job was to sneak into the Kingdom of Joy and Peace and turn the children back to their former lives at the CARNALville. One particular child was the target.

"The child known as Seeker," the dragon-clowns had spoken to Itsalmine in low voices. "Find something...anything...and make him want it more than he wants the King. The other children will soon follow him back here to Selfishness."

Now, in the early morning shadows, Itsalmine crept toward Seeker's home in the Village of Peace and Harmony near the castle. As he neared the Kingdom borders, Itsalmine considered his plan.

I will find something that is already important to the boy, he thought, something that he wants very much. Then, all I have to do is make him want it more!

The nasty little dragon rubbed his claws together in anticipation, picked his nose thoughtfully, and laughed a quiet but very wicked laugh.

CHAPTER ONE

Seeker emptied the coins onto his bed and counted them one more time.

Fifteen! He almost had enough! Seeker carefully put the coins back into his money pouch. It was a special money pouch. He had made it himself from soft blue leather with a red drawstring. There was no other pouch like it in the world. Seeker clutched it tightly to his heart. Just one more coin and he would finally have the right amount!

Seeker wanted a bow and a quiver full of arrows. He knew exactly which set he wanted because he had cut a picture out of a catalog. It cost sixteen coins.

He kept the picture in the top drawer of his dresser in a special little white box.

Seeker loved to look at the picture of the bow and arrow set and then run around his room, shooting invisible dragons and singing a song he had made up:

Hit the bull's-eye!
I will be a mighty warrior
With my trusty bow and arrows
I will run with might toward the foe—oh—
Dragons to the left and dragons to the right
I won't be afraid to fight
I'll lift my bow and arrow in the air—there!
Hit the bull's-eye!

For many months, Seeker had been saving money. He had worked at odd jobs around the Village of Peace and Harmony, and sold pictures that he had drawn of his adventures in the Kingdom. The coins earned from all his hard work, plus a few coins he had received for his birthday, were kept safely in the blue leather pouch and hidden underneath his mattress.

No one, absolutely no one, knew about the fifteen coins. The money in the blue leather pouch was a secret and Seeker hadn't told any of his friends, or anyone in his family. His mother thought that he had spent his money. Seeker had asked and asked her to buy a bow and arrow set for him but her answer was always the same, "When you are older, Seeker, then you can have a bow and arrow

2

set. Perhaps someday you could even earn the money to buy it yourself."

And I DID earn the money myself! Seeker thought happily. Only one more coin to go! I just need sixteen coins to buy the best bow and quiver of arrows in the village! And then I can surprise everybody! Soon I will be a mighty warrior for the King! Thinking again about the catalog picture, Seeker lifted up an imaginary bow, set an imaginary arrow in it, and then let it fly. I'll lift my bow and arrow in the air—there! Hit the bull's-eye!

Seeker didn't realize that a nasty little dragon had watched him count the coins. He didn't realize that the nasty little dragon, Itsalmine, was now rubbing his claws together in delight and breathing selfish thoughts into Seeker's mind: All yours. Every coin is all yours.

"It's all mine," Seeker smiled happily. "Every coin is all mine."

You worked hard. You saved your money and you deserve every single coin.

"I worked hard. I saved my money and I deserve every single coin..."

You can get whatever you want...it's only fair and right...

"I can get whatever I want...it's only fair and right..."

And you deserve the very best!

"And I deserve the very best!"

The best bow and arrow set in the village!

"The best bow and arrow set in the village!"

Itsalmine moved closer and began to sing into Seeker's mind, *You have worked so hard, and you deserve the best; it's only fair and right—that you have more, not less....*

Seeker hummed and rocked back and forth, clutching the blue leather pouch to his chest dreamily. "I have worked so hard, and I deserve the best; it's only fair and right—that I have more, not less...." Seeker had no idea that a dragon hummed along with him, and that the dragon had grown a little bit bigger than he had been before...

"Seeker!" his mother's voice interrupted his thoughts. "Weren't you planning to meet your friends at the Big Rock by now?"

"Oh yeah! Thanks, Mom!"

Seeker and his friends were planning to meet at the rock near the base of the Straight and Narrow Path. Then they were going to the castle to spend time with the King. Quickly hiding the blue leather pouch beneath his mattress, Seeker ran out of the house, raced through the streets of Peace and Harmony, and came to a skidding halt at the foot of the Straight and Narrow Path.

5

CHAPTER TWO

"Sorry I'm late!" Seeker called to his friends, but they didn't answer him. HopeSo, KnowSo, and Yes; Giggles, Gladness, and Glee; and Dawdle and Slow were all gathered around Doodle and Do. Everyone looked worried. Seeker moved in closer to hear what they were saying.

"Please!" KnowSo exclaimed, "Tell us what's wrong! We want to KNOW!"

"You tell them, Doodle," said Do.

"No, you do it, Do!" responded Doodle.

C'mon, Doodle! Do it!" insisted Do.

"Oh, all right," Doodle agreed with a sigh. "I'll DO it."

Doodle turned to their friends. "It's our big brother, Daring. He's been in the King's service across the sea and it's been months and months since we've seen him! Now he's close to home—his ship is anchored along the coast about twenty miles north of Royal Harbor. He's only going to be there for a few days and we REALLY want to go see him; but we can't!"

"Why can't you?" asked the children. This time, Do answered. "Well, Mom and Dad are going to go tomorrow,

7

but we don't have enough money for all of us to go," he said sadly. "This morning Mom told us that we need at least another fifteen coins to pay for all of us to travel and stay overnight..."

"Fifteen coins?!" Seeker echoed in surprise.

The dragon Itsalmine had been hiding quietly, but now quickly moved close to Seeker. *Yours! The coins are yours! You don't have to give them up!* he breathed.

"Mine," Seeker whispered to himself. "The money is mine...It's all mine. I have worked so hard, and I deserve the best; it's only fair and right—that I have more, not less.....!"

The words raced through his mind while the other children discussed possible solutions for Doodle and Do's problem.

Then KnowSo exclaimed, "I KNOW! Let's go and talk to the King about Doodle and Do's problem! He will know what to do!"

"Yes!" everyone agreed. "The King will know what to do!" And off they ran up the Straight and Narrow Path toward the castle. Seeker didn't run. He walked, slowly and thoughtfully, not realizing that he was listening to the voice of a dragon.

"I have worked so hard, and I deserve the best; it's only fair and right—that I have more, not less...."

Once Seeker was well on his way, Itsalmine hid behind a tree, happily realizing that he had grown again. Now he was a little larger and a little stronger than he had been. He stood picking his nose.

"Dragons aren't allowed within the castle walls," he mumbled to himself, "Unless, of course...unless someone happens to open a door!"

He laughed a wicked little laugh and waited.

9

CHAPTER THREE

When the children arrived at the castle courtyard, the King was there to meet them.

"King!" they cried, "Doodle and Do have a problem!"

"I know," responded the King,

"They need fifteen coins so they can go see their brother," explained HopeSo.

"I know," the King said again.

The King put his great arms around Doodle and Do's shoulders and bent down on one knee to look into their eyes. "DO you trust me?" he asked the young boys. When they nodded a determined yes, the King said, "Will you continue to trust me, even if your problem is very, very big?" he asked quietly.

The other children had been watching. They smiled at each other. No problem was too big for the King!

"We'll trust you, King!" said Doodle.

Do nodded. "Even if our very big problem is called fifteen coins, we'll trust you, King!"

The boys looked at each other, smiled and spoke together, "It's what we're going to DO!"

The King laughed and hugged them close. Then he stood up, turned to the other children, and said, "Come on everybody; today I want to take you to one of my favorite places!"

The children cheered and grabbed hold of the King's hands. "Wh-wh-where are we g-g-going, King?" asked Dawdle.

"A-a-are we g-g-going on an adventure, King?" asked Slow.

The children loved going on adventures in the Kingdom. "Are we going to fight some dragons today, King?" Seeker asked excitedly. He was remembering how they had rescued a whole village from the great dragon Greed.

11

The King smiled a mysterious smile. "There are many kinds of dragons, Seeker. And some of the greatest battles are fought right in here." The King gently touched Seeker's heart. The King's touch was hot, so hot that Seeker pulled away in surprise. An uncomfortable knot formed in his stomach and he couldn't look at the King's eyes.

The other children tugged at the King, "Let's get going to your favorite place!" Glee said. "Where is it?"

The King laughed. "It's just down that walkway over there. Do you see that hall that's extra shiny?"

Giggles laughed. "Extra shiny means extra slippery!"

The King laughed, too, and took his shoes off. "I'll race you!" he called; and off they went.

Usually Seeker was the one of the best at sliding down the shining Kingdom halls and walkways, but today he didn't feel like sliding or playing. He felt like thinking about his money.

Fifteen coins...So what if Doodle and Do need fifteen coins, and I just happen to have fifteen coins?! The King will look after Doodle and Do. It's not my problem.

The very moment when Seeker decided to think like that, a door someplace in the castle wall was opened. It was just the right size for the wicked dragon, Itsalmine, to squeeze through. He immediately began to breathe thoughts in Seeker's direction....

12

I worked hard for my money and it's all mine, Seeker thought. *It's all mine! And I can spend it on whatever I want...*

I have worked so hard, and I deserve the best; it's only fair and right—that I have more, not less....

Seeker walked slowly. Thoughts of the CARNALville of Selfishness, where he and the other children used to spend many of their days, began to form in his mind. Seeker hadn't thought about that place for a long time. *I could even use my money to play at the CARNALville,* Seeker thought to himself, *It wasn't such a bad place. The candy sure was good...Yeah... The special secret recipe candy....It sure was good...*

The dragon Itsalmine came even closer, growing a bit larger with each step. Seeker said aloud, "Maybe I should forget about the bow and arrow set for awhile and go visit the CARNALville. That stuff about being a mighty warrior was dumb anyway. I could never be a mighty warrior...I could never really hit the bull's-eye." Seeker licked his lips dreamily. "Hmm...I sure could go for just one little piece of that CARNALville candy...I haven't had any for so long..."

"Seeker! What are you DOing?" Doodle yelled as he came running toward his friend. "Hurry! The King is going to take us inside the White Tower! Hurry!"

"The White Tower?" Seeker echoed. "Uh..."

13

The dragon Itsalmine pulled, unseen, at Seeker's arm, whispering and drooling, "CARNALville candy…yummy, yummy CARNALville candy…"

"Uh…" Seeker said again.

"What's wrong with you, Seeker?" asked Doodle. "You know how much we've been wanting to get into that tower!"

The White Tower in the far corner of the castle gardens had been especially interesting to the children because it was locked. Every other place in the Kingdom was open to them, but each time they had tried to turn the handle on that one little tower, it refused to turn.

"Hurry, Seeker!" Doodle said again. "Come on!"

"Uh…Uh…Okay, I guess so." Seeker turned to go with his friend. The dragon tried to reach out his foot and trip Seeker, but it didn't work. (Dragon powers are very limited inside the castle walls.) Itsalmine stomped his feet and pouted. *Oh, well. Seeker would have to wait. He had something else he needed to do right now anyway…*

14

CHAPTER FOUR

At the White Tower, Seeker and his friends looked with great surprise at the wooden door. Some letters had appeared right in the center it!

*"I AM THE TOWER OF
KNOWLEDGE,
AND GREAT DESIRE IS MY KEY.
IF YOU REALLY WANT TO,
YOU CAN GET MY KEY FROM
THE KING!"*

The children turned excitedly to the King. "Is this your favorite place, King?" asked Gladness.

The King nodded. "ONE of my favorites!"

15

"DO we really get to go in here?" asked Doodle.

"DO you have the key? Do you? Do you, King?" Do and the others tugged at the King's hands.

"A key? Let's see, it should be here somewhere." The King smiled mysteriously and searched through his pockets.

The children waited patiently, and the King realized that he needed to give them a hint. "The key is actually the answer to my favorite question!" He folded his arms, leaned forward and winked. "Do you REALLY want to go in there?"

The children laughed. Of course! Here in the Kingdom, the only way you got into places was by REALLY wanting to! They all said together, "YES! We REALLY want to!"

Immediately, the King pulled a beautiful golden key from his pocket. Very slowly, he put the key into the lock, turned it, and the door swung open.

The children looked around with big eyes, their mouths open in amazement. There were doors and stairways, doors and stairways, and more doors and more stairways—hundreds and hundreds of doors and stairways! "Wow..." Seeker whispered, "how can all of this fit into one little tower?!"

16

KnowSo was very impressed. "Now I KNOW why this is one of your favorite places, King!" he said.

The children quickly began to explore. They ran up flights of stairs and then slid down the banisters, winding their way through each level. They slid down the shining hallways, across great balconies, and past countless doorways.

Above each door was a sign. Most of the words were difficult for the children to read. Many were blurry. Doodle and Do had been busily climbing to the highest level in the tower. They read the sign above the highest door. "King!" they called down to him. "We just read the sign above this door. It says, 'Doorway to My Father's Kingdom.' What does that mean?"

The King laughed and called out, "It means 'Doorway to My Father's Kingdom!'"

"King!" Doodle cried, "DO you have a dad?"

"Can we see him, King, can we?"

"Someday, when it is time, I will take you there myself to meet him. But right now, I want you all to come close to me. I have something special to show you."

Doodle and Do slid together down a series of banisters, talking excitedly. "The King is even better than I always thought he was!" said Doodle.

Do agreed, "He's amazing! Just think—all this inside one little tower!"

Doodle leaned over and whispered to his brother, "DO you think the King can fix our big problem with one little answer?"

Do giggled, "Yes, I DO!"

In the center of the Tower of Knowledge, on a glistening cabinet, was a book trimmed with gold. Light was shining out from its pages. As the children crowded around, the King said, "This is my book...the Great Book." The children peered into the pages and read aloud, "'Thee, thou, hitherto, wherefore'"...Glee shook her head, looked up, and said, "King, we don't understand these big words!"

The King smiled another of his mysterious smiles and answered, "Then I will open your eyes so that you can!" He stretched out his great hands and gently touched the children's eyes. When they looked again at the Great Book, they could understand the words. The King held the book open for them as they read page after page...

Seeker pointed at the first page excitedly. "Look! This is where the world came from!"

"Wow!" the other children said together.

"Yes!" Yes said, pointing at the next page. "This is where the birds came from, and the animals, and the people!"

"Wow!" the other children said together.

"Look at this!" cried HopeSo. "Look at all these stories! This is about a flood, and a big, big boat!"

The King continued opening the pages and the children continued with their excited comments. "Look what this person did...look what this person did...ooh, look what that person did!"

They looked farther and farther through the pages of the book. Then Seeker pointed and said, "King, here are some words I don't understand. It says, 'Whoever saves his life, will lose it...and whoever loses his life will find it.' What does it mean—if you find your life you lose it; and if you lose your life, you find it?"

The King's eyes twinkled. "Would you like me to tell you what the words mean, or *show* you what the words mean? My messenger will take you..."

Just then, HopeSo pointed at the book and cried out, "Look, King! The book talks about a man who sounds just like you!"

Everyone forgot about Seeker's question as the King answered HopeSo. "Really?" he asked with interest.

"Yes!" Yes nodded excitedly. "There are stories in here about a man who likes children and does great things and has a Kingdom!"

Giggles giggled. "He sounds just like you, King!"

"Really?" the King said again.

"B-b-but look what happened to the man!" Dawdle exclaimed.

"They wh-wh-whipped him…and did really m-m-mean things to him…" Slow said slowly.

"And then they put nails into his hands and feet…and he died!" HopeSo whispered.

Giggles sadly shook her head and whispered, "They took his life away."

Doodle was horrified. "Why did they DO that? Why would they take his life away like that?!"

Everyone was thoughtful and quiet, then the King spoke softly. "Perhaps they didn't take his life away!"

The children looked up at the King. He was smiling the most mysterious smile they had ever seen. "Perhaps," he said even more softly, "Perhaps he gave his life…willingly."

A sense of wonder filled the children's hearts. "Why would he DO something like that, King?" Do asked.

The King's smile deepened. "He would do it...He would give his life, because he knew it was the only way to open the door."

Seeker and his friends were puzzled. "Door? What door?"

The King looked up at the highest door in the Tower of Knowledge. "That door!"

Doodle and Do looked at each other, and then at the King. "Doorway to My Father's Kingdom?!"

All of the children turned together and looked at the King. He met their eyes for a moment, then looked down. The children followed the King's gaze...down to his big hands that were holding open the pages of the Great Book. Two faded old scars were on his hands; so faded that the children had never noticed them before.

KnowSo gasped. "You are the man in the book!"

Seeker nodded, "They didn't take your life from you...you gave it up!"

The King laughed. It was a joyful laugh that came from deep inside himself. "Yes! I gave my life and because I did, you can have life! Someday, when it is the right time, each of you who believes in me will go through the door

22

to my father's Kingdom…and what awaits you there is far greater than anything that you have ever dreamed or imagined!"

Yes moved closer to the King. Her eyes filled up with tears as she gently took both of the King's hands in her own. She very tenderly stroked the old faded scars and then kissed them. "Thank you, King," she whispered. "Thank you for giving your life…for us."

The other children crowded in closer to the King, hugging him and gently patting his hands. "Thank you, King. Thank you." Love for the King filled their hearts. They had loved him before, but now they really loved him.

After many long moments, Seeker whispered, "Whoever saves his life, will lose it…and whoever loses his life will find it." He looked up at the King. "Those were the words I started to ask you about before. You were just about to explain…you said…"

The King's eyes twinkled. "I said, 'Would you like me to tell you what the words mean, or *show* you what the words mean?'"

Suddenly, on the other side of the Tower of Knowledge, a door burst open; and a Messenger came in. He was very, very old, but very, very young at the same time. He was dressed in a royal tunic and carried a scroll and a golden trumpet. He bowed deeply to the King and asked, "Now?"

23

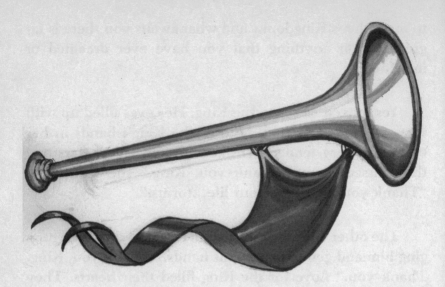

"Now!" laughed the King. He turned to the children. "Go with my Messenger. He will show you what the words from the Great Book mean!"

The Messenger blew his golden trumpet and then sang:

"Hear ye, hear ye, hear ye—
A story from the book!
Open your ears to hear it;
Open up your eyes and look."

The children happily joined in the Messenger's song and followed him...out the door through which he had just entered...

CHAPTER FIVE

Suddenly, the children were standing on a hill they had never seen before. Tall grasses waved in the wind and a blue lake sparkled at the base of the hill. The Tower of Knowledge had disappeared.

"Wh-wh-where are we?" Dawdle and Slow wondered.

"I've never seen this hill before...and I've never seen that lake, either," Yes said, standing closer to Seeker.

"Was the wind blowing today, KnowSo?" Seeker whispered.

"No, it wasn't," KnowSo whispered back.

"This is very peculiar!" Giggles giggled nervously.

"How can all this fit inside one little tower?" Glee asked the question that each of the children was wondering.

"I'd like to KNOW how that door can just stand there by itself!" KnowSo said, looking back at the door they had come through and shaking his head in wonder. The other children looked at the door and shook their heads, too.

But there was no more time to wonder, because the Messenger was still singing and leading them across the hill...

The children followed the Messenger until they reached a spot where they could look over the other side of the hill. There the Messenger stopped, put one finger to his lips to quiet the children, and then pointed. Coming toward them was a crowd of people.

The children sank down into the grass, and watched as the crowd came closer. The people were dressed differently than they had ever seen before. There were lots of children skipping and playing as they climbed the hill, but a few of them had to be carried. Seeker and his friends noticed then that many of the people were sick or crippled; and they realized that the whole crowd was following one man.

"Look at that man!" Giggles pointed and whispered. "He looks just like the King! He..."

Gladness stopped his sister. "That man doesn't just LOOK like the King..."

"That man IS the King." The children whispered together in amazement. They turned their heads toward the Messenger who was smiling at them.

"What is this place?" KnowSo asked. "Where are we?"

"And who are YOU, anyway?" HopeSo asked.

"I am the King's Messenger!" He bowed slightly and smiled again. "When you REALLY want to understand something from the Great Book, I will be there to bring it to life for you!"

KnowSo nodded, "I get it—when we REALLY wanted to know what it means to 'lose your life and FIND it'..."

The Messenger smiled and said, "The King told me to bring you here...inside this story from the Great Book. Now, open up your eyes...and look." He pointed back toward the people and the man on the hill.

They all watched silently as the Man took some children from the crowd up onto his knees and hugged them. The children that were being carried were laid down at his feet. Seeker and his friends watched in wonder as the Man reached out and touched those children, and within moments they stood up, totally well!

"Wow!" Seeker and the others whispered.

Then someone brought a blind man to the man, and he healed the blind man so he could see. He healed the cripples so they could walk and he healed the sick people so they were well. Every person the man touched was very, very happy. The whole crowd began to cheer and jump up and down and hug each other.

Then, in the midst of all that happiness, a young man wearing rich-looking clothes and shining jewels rode up the hill on a camel. Servants helped him get onto the ground and then bowed low as he passed them and pushed his way through the crowd. He stood proudly in front of the man on the hill.

"Oooh..." said Giggles, giggling. "He sure must be somebody important!"

Glee nodded, "Or at least, he *thinks* he is somebody important!"

"I'm sure GLAD I don't have to get around on a camel!" Gladness said, holding his nose.

Suddenly, Do pointed, "Yuck! DO you see it?"

"See what?" the others asked.

"DO you see the dragon?"

"Dragon?!" the other children sat up taller and strained to see.

28

"I see it," Giggles said, not giggling. "There—right behind that rich guy! Oh yuck! It's picking its nose!"

"That is so disgusting!" Yes cried, moving closer to Seeker.

Hiding very closely behind the rich man, so closely that he could hardly be seen, was the wicked little dragon, Itsalmine. Except now, he was not little...he was enormous! The rich man had been feeding the selfish dragon for many years.

"Good master," the rich man spoke loudly to the man on the hill, "what must I do to have eternal life?"

The man on the hill replied, "If you want to have eternal life, give up what you have to the poor and come and follow me!"

"Give up what you have?!" The dragon Itsalmine was so startled that he nearly stepped out from his hiding place! The dragon and the rich man shook their heads together stubbornly.

Then the rich young man reached inside his cloak, searching for something. A moment later he pulled out a little blue leather pouch tied with a red drawstring. Seeker looked at it—and gasped!

"Hey!" he called out loudly, standing to his feet. "That's my blue leather pouch! Where did you..."

Seeker couldn't finish the sentence because the other children pulled him back to the ground. "Shh! Sit down, Seeker!"

"Wh-Wh-What's the m-ma-matter, Seeker?" asked Dawdle.

"A-A-Are you okay?" Slow asked, concerned.

"That guy has my blue leather pouch! I made it myself! No one else could have one just like it!" Seeker struggled to get up again, and then realized the messenger was motioning for them to watch the scene before them.

The rich young man was still holding up the blue leather pouch. Suddenly the dragon leaned into him even more closely and spoke with convincing power, "You have worked so hard, and you deserve the best; it's only fair and right—that you have more, not less...."

The rich man echoed the dragon's words, "I have worked so hard, and I deserve the best; it's only fair and right—that I have more, not less...."

Seeker had turned very pale. "Those words," he whispered to himself. "Those words. I thought those exact words this morning after I counted my coins! And I've been singing those exact words all day long!"

Seeker watched as the rich young man held the blue leather pouch to his heart with one hand and patted the dragon with the other, his eyes never leaving the man's.

Moments passed and the children hardly breathed. What would happen? Would he do what the man asked?

"Oh, I get it!" KnowSo whispered. "Whosoever saves his life, will lose it...and whoever loses his life will find it!"

The other children turned questioningly. "What?"

"That's why we're here!" KnowSo whispered excitedly, "The messenger brought us here so we would really understand what those words mean! Don't you get it?!"

The children nodded and HopeSo said, "Yeah, I get it! I understand, and I sure hope that guy does!"

"Come on, rich guy!" Giggles whispered earnestly. "Make the right choice!"

Everyone joined Giggles in her whispered cheer. "Come on, rich guy! You can do it! Come on! Make the right choice! Give it up!"

More moments passed. Then the rich man cleared his throat. The children held their breath, but to their great disappointment, the rich man firmly and stubbornly shook his head. "It's all mine," he said, "and I can't give it up...not even for you." Then he turned and walked away.

And the man on the hill looked very, very sad.

Then the whole scene vanished. The crowd was gone, the rich man was gone, even the camel was gone. The children looked around, wondering, but nothing remained except the wind-blown grass on the hill. Then, to their amazement, the King was sitting in front of them on the hill...looking right at Seeker. The intense way that the King looked at him made Seeker feel uncomfortable, and he turned away. The knot inside his stomach had returned, now even tighter than before.

"I understand, King," KnowSo said as he ran to sit next to the King. "The words in the Great Book— 'Whoever saves his life, will lose it...and whoever loses his life will find it.' "

"Yes!" nodded Yes with excitement. "The rich young man wanted his money more than he wanted you, King!"

Gladness agreed. "So instead of really finding life, he lost it. That was a great story, King!"

"DO you think we can go back into the Tower now, King?" asked Doodle. "I want to look at that Great Book again!"

The King nodded toward the messenger, who led them back to the door that was still standing on the other side of the hill. The King and the messenger smiled at each other, and immediately the children were inside the Tower of Knowledge.

CHAPTER SIX

"I have a gift for you," the King said as he walked over to the glistening cabinet in the center of the Tower of Knowledge. The King opened a drawer and took out miniature copies of the Great Book. Every copy looked just like the Great Book, but smaller—so the children could actually carry the Book with them! The King gave one to each of the children. "Read from this Book every day," he said. "In it are the laws, the promises, the treasures of my Kingdom. Through its pages, you will get to know me better."

The King handed HopeSo and KnowSo their copies and said, "Look inside right now. You will

see a bookmark to help you remember what you learned today..."

"I get it!" KnowSo said, laughing. "Here are those words again: 'Whoever saves his life, will lose it...and whoever loses his life will find it!' "

"Wow," the children said, carefully flipping through the pages. "This is so awesome!"

When the King gave a copy of the Great Book to Doodle and Do, he said, "And, as you read my Book, you will realize that no problem is too big, even if it is a very, very big problem. You will learn to trust me."

"We will really trust you, King!" said Doodle.

Do nodded. "Even if our very big problem is called fifteen coins, we'll trust you!" The boys looked at each other, smiled and spoke together, "It's what we're going to DO!"

Seeker was watching. He watched as the King hugged Doodle and Do closely. *Fifteen coins*, Seeker thought again. *They need fifteen coins. I have fifteen coins in my blue leather pouch...at least, I thought I did. Maybe that rich guy in the story got into my room somehow and took my pouch! How could he have one exactly like it?*

At that very moment the King turned toward Seeker, smiled, and handed him a copy of the Great Book. "Reading my book will help you to make good choices and wise decisions, Seeker. It will help you to become a mighty warrior for me."

"Mighty warrior?" Seeker looked up, surprised. Then he turned away and shook his head. "Not me, King. I'll never be a mighty warrior."

The King put his hand on the boy's shoulder, but Seeker refused to look up. He was embarrassed to realize that his eyes had begun to fill with tears. He mumbled a *thank you* as he stuffed the book into his backpack and ran out of the Tower of Knowledge.

Seeker ran all the way down the Straight and Narrow Path, through the Village of Peace and Harmony, into his house, up the stairs, and into his bedroom. Frantically, he reached under his mattress and pulled out his blue leather pouch.

"It's still here! It wasn't my pouch that rich guy had after all! But, it was the same color, the same shape—I made this myself! No one could have one exactly like it!"

He opened the pouch and shook out the fifteen coins, counting them to be sure they were all there. "One, two, three...fifteen! Whew! Every single coin is still here!"

Very carefully, Seeker inspected the blue leather pouch. "I don't understand! How could that guy have exactly the same pouch as me? I don't get it!"

Seeker sat on his bed with a sigh. "Hmm...the King sure looked sad when that rich man wouldn't give it up and follow him. And the King sure looked sad at me when he sat on the hill. The King couldn't know about my fifteen coins...or could he? And if he does know...does he think I'm acting like that rich guy?" Seeker shivered. "What a scary thought!"

Other thoughts raced through Seeker's mind as he gathered the coins up and put them back inside the pouch.

"Doodle and Do really need fifteen coins. I want Doodle and Do to be happy; I want them to see their brother. But I REALLY want a bow and arrow! I want to be a mighty warrior!" Thinking again about the catalog picture, Seeker lifted up an imaginary bow, but this time he lifted it more slowly than usual. Then he set an imaginary arrow in the bow, and let it fly, singing the words from his song more slowly than usual, "I'll lift my bow and arrow in the air—there...Hit the bull's-eye..."

As Seeker leaned back on his bed, his backpack fell open, and he noticed his copy of the Great Book poking out of the top. Seeker reached for it and opened it to where the King had placed the bookmark. *Whoever saves his life, will lose it; and whoever loses his life will find it,* Seeker read aloud. "Hmm..."

The wicked dragon Itsalmine had been watching. The situation had seemed pretty well under control—until now. "Not the Book!" Itsalmine was startled to see it. "Not THE Book! Yikes! This calls for action!"

He quickly slithered out from his hiding place and whispered, *Those words from the book have nothing to do with you, Seeker. It's just a book! And Doodle and Do's problem is not your problem. The King will look after them.*

"Doodle and Do's problem isn't my problem," Seeker said. "The King will look after them."

The dragon moved closer. *The King has lots of money. He wouldn't want you to give up your fifteen little coins.*

Seeker leaned back on his bed thoughtfully, "The King has lots of money. He wouldn't want me to give up my fifteen little coins."

Itsalmine whispered with convincing power, *You have worked so hard, and you deserve the best; it's only fair and right—that you have more, not less....*

Seeker sat straight up and looked around. "Those words! That voice! It's the dragon! Hey! Where are you, you ugly nose-picking thing?" Seeker raced around his room, searching under his bed and in his closet.

Itsalmine tried to escape Seeker's search, all the while trying to get his attention. *You deserve a bow and arrow set!*

Seeker clenched his teeth. "If I had a bow and arrow set right now, I know what I'd do with it! I would get you,

you...But wait... I can't even see you! A bow and arrow wouldn't do any good."

Just then, a picture flashed through Seeker's mind. He saw the rich young man holding the blue leather pouch to his chest and turning away from the King. Then Seeker heard again the words the King spoke when he gave him his copy of the Great Book, "Reading my Book will help you to make good choices and wise decisions. It will help , you to become a mighty warrior for me!"

Seeker laughed out loud and took hold of the Great Book. "I get it! I understand now! I can get rid of this dragon by making the right choice! I can be a mighty warrior right now—right here, right this very minute!"

Itsalmine was frantic. *Remember the CARNALville candy! Yummy, special secret recipe CARNALville candy! You can make a good choice, kid—you can choose to use, your money to buy candy for all your friends! That would be a nice thing to do! Come on kid...*

Seeker shut his ears to the voice. Closing his eyes tightly and holding his Great Book close, Seeker took a deep breath and shouted boldly, "I choose to lose my life. I choose to give up what I want to do and I choose to do what is right!"

Itsalmine moaned as if he had been wounded. He shrank to the same size he had been when he came to Seeker's life.

"I don't want to lose out like that rich guy!" Seeker shouted. "I will give up my money; I will give my fifteen coins to Doodle and Do!"

Itsalmine shrank even smaller as he roared in pain and left the room. The miserable, nasty dragon cried and picked his nose all the way back to the CARNALville—all the way back to his master in the deep dark place beneath the trap door of Selfishness.

"Whew! That was intense!" Seeker sat down with a sigh of relief and smiled. "Doodle and Do, start packing your bags! You get to go and see your brother!"

He spilled the fifteen coins out onto his bed. "Now, let's see. If I just give the coins to Doodle and Do, they

might not want to take them from me; or they might feel like they would have to pay me back...."

Seeker stood up and paced back and forth, trying to decide what to do. "Somehow," he said to himself, "it's got to be a secret...it's got to be a mystery. Yeah! And it's got to be an adventure! I need to put the coins some place where Doodle and Do can find them...and in some kind of package that won't let them know who put them there!" He began searching in his closet for a container.

Then Seeker had an idea. He quickly opened his top dresser drawer where he kept the special little white box.

He looked inside at the catalog picture of the bow and arrow set. "That's strange," Seeker said aloud. "I used to think the bow in this picture was really shiny gold...but now, it doesn't look very shiny or very gold! And you only get two arrows with it! I never noticed that!" He laughed. "I think while I'm saving up my money again, I'll shop around for a better deal!"

Seeker crumpled up the picture and tossed it into his trash can. Then he put the fifteen coins into the box and tied it up with a string. "Now," he said, reaching for a pen, "I'll write real big and slanted so they won't recognize my hand writing!"

Very carefully Seeker wrote, "To Doodle and Do from....?" across the top of the box.

As he drew the question mark, *Seeker started feeling really, really, really excited. Nobody knows! Nobody will ever know!* he thought happily. *Doodle and Do will be able to see their brother, and no one will ever, ever know where the money came from, because it will be my secret.* He giggled and shook the box of jingling coins. "My most mysterious secret."

CHAPTER SEVEN

A few blocks from Seeker's home, not too far from the Big Rock at the base of the Straight and Narrow Path, Doodle and Do sat on their front porch. They had their hands propped under their chins thoughtfully. They were very serious. Not sad, not worried, just very serious. Tomorrow morning, their parents would be going to see Daring, and still, no sign of the fifteen coins. Doodle had just checked the mailbox again.

"Why DO you keep checking the mailbox?" Do asked.

Doodle shrugged his shoulders. "I don't know," he responded. "The King promised to look after us. He said that we could trust him, and that no problem is too big—not even a problem called fifteen coins."

Do looked at Doodle, trying not to laugh. "But DO you really think that's how the King will help us? DO you really think the fifteen coins will get here in the mailbox?"

Doodle shrugged. "It doesn't matter how the King gets them here. What matters is that we trust him! And even though it's hard to trust..."

Then both boys smiled, and their serious mood left them as they said together, "It's what we're going to DO!" Laughing, they went into their house.

Meanwhile, Seeker ran down the stairs, out from his house, and through the village streets toward Doodle and Do's home.

A tall hedge bordered their yard. "Perfect!" Seeker thought as he crept along beside the hedge. When he reached the gate of Doodle and Do's yard he peeked out, carefully making sure that no one was there to see him. Excitement seemed ready to burst inside Seeker as he tiptoed up to the mailbox, then very carefully and very quietly set the little white box inside.

Seeker could hardly keep from laughing as he pictured Doodle and Do discovering the mysterious little package in their mailbox. He struggled to keep quiet as he crept back around the corner of the hedge and...bumped into...

...the King.

"Oh!" Seeker cried in surprise, then quickly composed himself. "Oh, hello there, King! So, uh, what are you doing here in the village, today?"

The King smiled one of his most mysterious smiles, and said, "I had to come down and say *thank you* to someone."

"Oh. Who did you have to say thank you to?" asked Seeker. "What for?"

The King looked around to make sure no one was listening. Then he whispered, "I had to come and say thank you for fifteen coins in a little white box tied up with a string." The King smiled, leaned forward, and winked at Seeker.

Seeker could hardly believe his ears. "King! That's my most mysterious secret! You won't tell anyone, will you, King? Will you? How did you know, anyway?"

The King led Seeker over to the Big Rock at the base of the Straight and Narrow Path. "Seeker, you will find out, as you read your copy of the Great Book, that whenever you give something away that REALLY matters to you—you've actually given it to Me."

"I have?" Seeker said.

The King nodded as he sat down on the Big Rock.

"Listen closely, Seeker," the King said. "There is a battle every day—whether to seek to keep your life, or give it to me. The inner battle of your heart is the hardest battle you will ever fight, Seeker, and no one sees that war except for me. And *I* say that you are a mighty warrior!"

"I am?" Seeker asked in surprise.

Then the King did something that *really* surprised Seeker. He stood behind him, turned him toward the village, and put his big hands over Seeker's hands. Then together, they lifted up an imaginary bow, set an imaginary arrow in it, pulled back the string, and aimed.

Suddenly, with the King's help, Seeker was able to see Doodle and Do's front porch. He could see Doodle coming out from their house and going to check the mailbox...just one more time. Seeker watched Doodle open the door of the mailbox, and he watched the boy's surprise when he saw the package. Seeker could hear Doodle call to his brother, Do, to come and look at the strange little white box.

Seeker felt the King's arms, strong around his; and he felt the King pull back the invisible arrow...just a bit farther. "Ready, Seeker?" the King whispered. Seeker nodded, his eyes filling with happy tears.

They pulled back the arrow just a little bit more, and then, with a surge of strength and power like Seeker had never felt before, they let go. "Hit the bull's-eye!" the King whispered with laughter in his voice.

The invisible arrow hit the little white box exactly the same moment that Doodle and Do untied the string, and fifteen coins fell out into their hands.

The King wrapped his great arms around Seeker, and together they watched the two happy boys talking excitedly about how the King had solved their big problem in one little answer—a little white box tied up with a string! They listened as Doodle and Do wondered how the little box actually got into their mailbox; they talked about getting to see their brother.

"We get to see Daring! We really DO!"

"Time to start packing for the trip, Doodle!"

"It's what we're going to DO!"

Then Doodle and Do turned and ran up the walk and into their house to tell their parents the good news.

Seeker looked up at the King, and his eyes were shining. "We hit the bull's-eye, King!" The King nodded.

Then Seeker took both of the King's hands and touched the old faded scars. "That's what you did, isn't it, King?" Seeker said quietly, "You really hit the bull's-eye! You didn't keep your life. You gave it up and you really found it!"

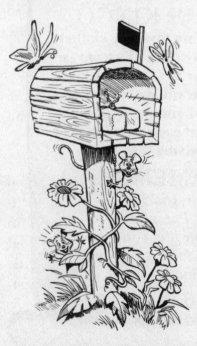

The King smiled another of his mysterious smiles. Then he and Seeker turned and walked together through the streets of Peace and Harmony in his Kingdom.

You might be wondering what happened to Doodle and Do and their brother, Daring; and whether or not Seeker ever got a bow and arrow set...well, that's another adventure in the Kingdom.

THINK ABOUT THE STORY

The King is the man in the book. He has a name. Do you know what it is? His name is Jesus. The Great Book also has a name. The words in the Bible will help you get to know King Jesus; and your life will really be a never-ending adventure!

SEARCH THE PAGES OF THE GREAT BOOK (THE BIBLE)

Matthew 19:16-22: The story of the Rich Young Ruler
Matthew 6:3,4: Now that's an adventure!
Matthew 6:19-21: Treasures forever

TALK TO THE KINGÖ

"King Jesus, sometimes my toys, my clothes, my money and all my STUFF seem so important to me. Help me to see what REALLY matters. Help me be willing to give and to share cheerfully whenever I get the chance! And I know that each time I give to someone, I'm REALLY giving it to you!"

VERSE TO REMEMBERÖ

Matthew 16:25
(Hugga-Wugga™ Paraphrase)
If you seek to keep your life, you'll lose it, lose it; But give your life to Jesus and life you'll find!

Matthew 16, (clap) verse 25!

Land of Laws Forgotten

GENEROSITY

CARNALVILLE

Valley of Lost Dreams

World Beyond
the Kingdom

Island of Despair

ROYAL HARBOR

Talking Tree Forest

The Kingdom
of
Joy and Peace

N
E
W
S

The Adventure in the Kingdom™
by Dian Layton

SEEKER'S GREAT ADVENTURE

Seeker and his friends leave the CARNALville of Selfishness and begin the great adventure of really knowing the King!

RESCUED FROM THE DRAGON

The King needs an army to conquer a very disgusting dragon and rescue the people who live in the Village of Greed.

SECRET OF THE BLUE POUCH

The children of the Kingdom explore the pages of an ancient golden book and step through a most remarkable doorway — into a brand new kind of adventure!

IN SEARCH OF WANDERER

Come aboard the sailing ship, "The Adventurer," and find out how Seeker learns to fight dragons through the window of the Secret Place.

THE DREAMER

Moira, Seeker's older sister, leaves the Kingdom and disappears into the Valley of Lost Dreams. Can Seeker rescue his sister before it's too late?

ARMOR OF LIGHT

In the World Beyond the Kingdom, Seeker must use the King's weapons to fight the dragons Bitterness and Anger to save the life of one young boy.

CARRIERS OF THE KINGDOM

Seeker and his friends discover that the Kingdom is within them! In the Land of Laws Forgotten they meet with Opposition, and the children battle against some very nasty dragons who do not want the people to remember...

Available at your local Christian bookstore.

For more information and sample chapters, visit www.destinyimage.com